Chris RIDDELL

Ottoline goes to School

MACMILLAN CHILDREN'S BOOKS

For my sister, Lynn

Chapter One

Ottoline lived in Apartment 243 of the P. W. HUFFLEDINCK TOWER, which everybody called the Pepperpot Building because it looked like one.

THE PEPPERPOT BUILDING

THE POINTY TOWER

APARTMENT 243

THE SHOEBOX BUILDING

THE ICE-CREAM CONE BUILDING

Ottoline

LIKES SOLVING TRICKY PROBLEMS AND WORKING OUT CLEVER PLANS IN HER NOTEBOOK

PETTIGREW PARK AND ORNAMENTAL GARDENS

Her parents were Collectors who travelled around the world. They were hardly ever at home, but Ottoline was well looked after and she was never lonely. And besides, she had her best friend, Mr. Munroe, for company.

Jean-Pierre

FROM THE HOME-COOKED MEAL Cº

Pete

FROM McBEAN'S CLEANING SERVICE

Kate and Teresa

FROM SMITH & SMITH PILLOW-PLUMPING AND CURTAIN-DRAWING TECHNICIANS

Madame Wong

FROM THE SMILING DRAGON CLOTHES-FOLDING Cº

Geraldine and Geraldine

FROM HAPPY NEST BED MAKERS

Marion

FROM MARION'S BATHROOM SUPPLIES

Mr. Munroe

FROM NORWAY

Big Doug

FROM DOOR-HANDLE SHINERS INC.

The Guys

FROM THE 1,000-STRONG LIGHTBULB CHANGING Cº

Although Ottoline's parents were away
a lot, they always kept in touch with
postcards.

Greetings
from the
NOME ELK-DECORATING
FESTIVAL

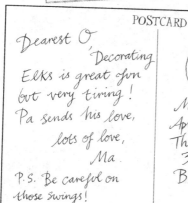

POSTCARD

Dearest O,
'Decorating
Elks is great fun
but very tiring!
Pa sends his love,
lots of love,
Ma.
P.S. Be careful on
those swings!
xxx

NORTH
★ 22.2.08 ★
WOODS

22¢

Miss O. Brown,
Apt. 243,
The Pepperpot Bld.
3rd Street,
BIG CITY 3001

OTTOLINE WRITES TO HER PARENTS
BY SENDING LETTERS TO THE
ROVING COLLECTORS' SOCIETY.
THEY MAKE SURE ROVING COLLECTORS
GET THEIR POST NO MATTER WHERE
IN THE WORLD THEY HAPPEN TO BE.

MONDAY
SUNGLASSES

TUESDAY
COAT

WEDNESDAY
DUNGAREES

THURSDAY
EAR MUFFS

FRIDAY
JUMPER

FRIDAY

SATURDAY
SUN HAT

SUNDAY
SILLY GLASSES

(INDOORS
ONLY)

OTTOLINE WAS
WEARING HER
TUESDAY COAT.
SHE HAD A SPECIAL
ITEM OF CLOTHING
FOR EACH DAY
OF THE WEEK

One morning Ottoline and Mr. Munroe
were taking a walk in Pettigrew Park and
Ornamental Gardens. It was a Tuesday, and
on Tuesday mornings they liked to visit the
turtles in the Turtle Pool . . .

... which is where they met Cecily Forbes-Lawrence III and her Patagonian pony, Mumbles.

EAST CROYDON MARSHMALLOW TREE

NORFOLK SNAFFLER

EAST AFRICAN TUFTY SHRUB

"I like your pony," said Ottoline.

"Thank you," said Cecily. "Mumbles is from Patagonia, you know. I like your dog."

"That's not a dog," laughed Ottoline. "That's Mr. Munroe."

Ottoline and Cecily fed the turtles stale crackers that Mr. Munroe had brought especially, and Cecily told Ottoline a fascinating story about a boy with feet so enormous that he could use them as a sunshade.

THE BOY WITH ENORMOUS FEET

"... and then Rupert became the world junior hopscotch champion, but that's another story," said Cecily. "I must go now. Mumbles's mane needs brushing."

"Can I help?" asked Ottoline excitedly. She loved brushing hair. Mr. Munroe didn't.

"Maybe some other time," said Cecily, walking off in the direction of the ornamental maze. "By the way, your dog's coat needs brushing too."

"She seems nice," said Ottoline, after Cecily had gone. Mr. Munroe didn't say anything.

The next day Ottoline met Cecily on the
ornamental bridge.

They played Pooh Sticks with twigs that
Mr. Munroe had found especially.

Cecily told Ottoline all about her Great-
Uncle Oscar, the misunderstood pirate.

"... and in the end he had four parrots, two on each shoulder, but they were no help when his trousers caught fire, but that's another story," said Cecily. "I must go now. I've got to take Mumbles to his showjumping class."

"Can I watch?" asked Ottoline excitedly. Mr. Munroe didn't have any classes. He was too shy.

"Maybe some other time," said Cecily, walking off in the direction of the bonsai-tree forest. "Your dog's dropped your umbrella."

"I like her," said Ottoline after Cecily had gone. "She tells amazing stories."

Mr. Munroe didn't hear her. He was busy fishing the umbrella out of the ornamental stream.

He got very wet.

The next day Ottoline met Cecily in the park . . .

. . . and the next day . . .

. . . and the next.

"... and all they found was a skeleton wearing a blue polka-dot bow tie," said Cecily.

"Incredible," said Ottoline. "I must go now. Mr. Munroe doesn't like the rain, and it's almost teatime."

"Can I come?" asked Cecily.

"Of course you can, Cecily," said Ottoline excitedly. "Mr. Munroe and I would like that very much, wouldn't we, Mr. Munroe?"

Mr. Munroe didn't say anything.

Ottoline didn't notice. She was busy catching up with Cecily, who was walking off in the direction of the Pepperpot Building.

Chapter Two

Ottoline and Cecily had tea on the Beidermeyer sofa.

Cecily told Ottoline about her family. Her father was somebody extremely important in the Big City Bank. He had meetings all day long, and when he came home he would have more meetings about the meetings he was going to have the next day. His secretary was called Miss Hopkins and she arranged his meetings.

MISS HOPKINS

MUMBLES HAD A SAUCER OF MILK

CECILY PUT A SAUCER DOWN FOR MR. MUNROE

If Cecily wanted her father to read her a bedtime story she had to arrange it with Miss Hopkins well in advance, so usually she didn't bother.

OTTOLINE WAS VERY IMPRESSED WITH THE WAY CECILY SIPPED HER TEA

A DOUBLE-SPOUTED TEAPOT FROM OTTOLINE'S PARENTS' TEAPOT COLLECTION

Cecily's mother was somebody extremely important in the Big City Museum of Modern Art. She went to parties almost every night. When she wasn't going to other people's parties she was having parties of her own. Her secretary was called Miss Dickinson and she arranged her parties. If Cecily wanted her mother to tuck her up in bed she had to arrange it with Miss Dickinson well in advance, so usually she didn't bother.

MISS DICKINSON

". . . of course, I'm fine about it," said Cecily. "But it's Mumbles I feel sorry for. Mother and Father are just too busy to take any notice of him, and Patagonian ponies can be very sensitive, you know."

"Can they? How fascinating," said Ottoline, pouring them another cup. "We should do this more often."

"I'm afraid I can't," said Cecily. "Mumbles and I have to go back to school next week."

"School?" said Ottoline.

"Yes," said Cecily. "The Alice B. Smith School for the Differently Gifted."

"It sounds like fun," said Ottoline.

"It isn't," said Cecily firmly. "By the way, where has your dog got to?"

Mr. Munroe was up on the roof of the Pepperpot Building, which is where he often went when he was sad. Ottoline was his best friend and he didn't want to share her.

Ever since Professor and Professor Brown had found him in a bog in Norway and brought

him back to live with them, Mr. Munroe and Ottoline had been inseparable.

They had had all sorts of adventures together . . .

Like the time they found
themselves at sea . . .

YOU CAN
READ ALL ABOUT
IT IN "OTTOLINE
AT SEA"

. . . and the time they caught the notorious
jewel thief the Yellow Cat . . .

YOU CAN
READ ALL ABOUT
IT IN "OTTOLINE
AND THE YELLOW CAT"

But that's another story.

The sun came out and a warm breeze ruffled
Mr. Munroe's hair. The sun didn't come out

very often in the bog in Norway. It felt good
to be standing on the roof of the Pepperpot
Building instead of in a wet puddle in a cold
bog. It felt good to have Ottoline as his best
friend, and Cecily wasn't so bad. Not really.

When Mr. Munroe came down from the roof
Cecily and Mumbles had gone.

"Feeling better?" Ottoline asked.

Mr. Munroe nodded.

"Good," said Ottoline.
"I've got a clever plan!"

Mr. Munroe sat on the
Beidermeyer rocking
chair with a little sigh.

"I've just asked
Ma and Pa to send
us to school!"

Professor & Professor
Brown
c/o The Roving Collectors'
Society

Dear Ma and Pa,
                     I think it is time for
me to go to a proper school. My new friend
Cecily Forbes-Lawrence III goes to the
Alice B. Smith School for the Differently
Gifted and is very good at sipping tea.
Mr. Munroe and I would like to discover
our different gifts so we can help you
in your collecting when we grow up,
                lots of love,

P.S. I'm giving   x x x
this letter to Max
to deliver to the
society on his paper
round. Write back
soon!

OTTOLINE'S LETTER
TO HER PARENTS

Chapter Three

Two days later, Mr. Munroe found a
postcard and a brown-paper parcel on
the doormat.

Greetings
From the
Sarawak
Hornbill
Festival

POSTCARD

Dearest O,
           I'm so
pleased you've decided
that you'd like to go
to school. We've contacted
the Alice B. Smith
school and they were
delighted to accept you.
Pa sends his love,
        lots of love,
                Ma.
P.S. Your suitcase is
in the cupboard. XXX

RAIN
13·04·08
FOREST

Miss O Brown,
Apt. 243,
The Pepperpot Bld,
3rd Street,
BIG CITY 3001

Mr. Munroe took the postcard and the brown-paper parcel to Ottoline, who was busy arranging her Odd Shoe collection.

34

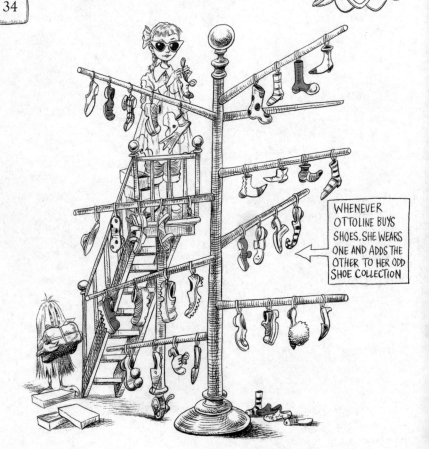

WHENEVER OTTOLINE BUYS SHOES, SHE WEARS ONE AND ADDS THE OTHER TO HER ODD SHOE COLLECTION

Ottoline read the postcard and then opened
the brown-paper parcel.

HAT

GYMSLIP

BLAZER

35

THESE WERE
IN THE PARCEL

TIE

SHIRTS

APRON

PYJAMAS

UNDERWEAR

MR. MUNROE KEPT
THE STRING TO ADD
TO THE BALL OF
STRING IN HIS
BEDROOM

"Thank you, Mr. Munroe,"
she said. "We must pack
straight away!"

When Ottoline opened the cupboard to get
her suitcase, a large bear stepped out.

EXTREMELY
SMALL
PAINTING

OLD
CURTAINS

"Hello," said Ottoline to the bear. "Would you mind handing me my suitcase?"

"Not at all," said the bear, rummaging in the cupboard. "Going somewhere nice?"

"I'm going to the Alice B. Smith School for the Differently Gifted!" said Ottoline with a big smile. "You can help me pack if you like."

"I'd be delighted," said the bear. "And I'll look after the apartment while you're away — I'm sure there's snow on the way."

THE BEAR HAD NEVER BEEN TO SCHOOL, BUT HE SEEMED TO KNOW EXACTLY WHAT TO PACK

39

THE PICNIC CLUB
IN THE WOODS
Admit one + a friend
FROM MIDNIGHT TILL LATE   BLACK TIE

THE BEAR WAS EXTREMELY WELL TRAVELLED SO WAS VERY GOOD AT PACKING SUITCASES

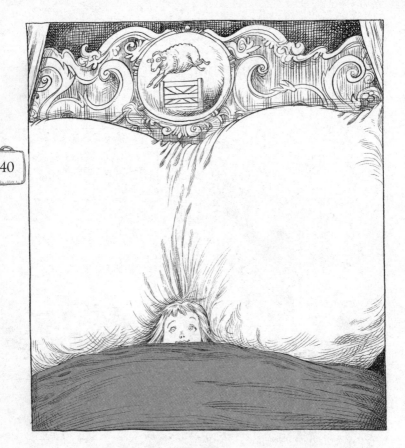

That night Ottoline was so excited she couldn't sleep. She had never been to school. Instead she did the lessons her mother and father, Professor and Professor Brown, sent her every week.

Sometimes they
were hard . . .

Sometimes they were
complicated . . .

And sometimes . . .

. . . they were fun.

Although Ottoline had lots of friends in the Big City . . .

THE BEAR FROM THE BASEMENT

VIVIENNE FROM THE 3RD ST SHOE STORE

MRS. PASTERNAK FROM APARTMENT 244 AND HER PET MONKEY, MORRIS

MAX THE PAPER BOY

MR. MUNROE

. . . she had never been to school, so she didn't have any school friends.

Ottoline couldn't wait to go to the Alice B. Smith School for the Differently Gifted with her new friend Cecily, which was why she was too excited to sleep.

Mr. Munroe didn't sleep much either.

Chapter Four

In the morning, Ottoline and Mr. Munroe said goodbye to the bear and walked to the bus stop on the corner of 3rd Street and Windmill.

A yellow school bus drew up.

"You must be Ottoline Brown," said the driver. "Hop in."

Ottoline climbed on to the yellow school bus. "Welcome aboard," said the driver. "I'm Alice B. Smith, and these are my gifted students." Alice B. Smith introduced everyone to Ottoline. There was Brian, the son of the Invisible Man, and his dog, Bodge. Then the Wright sisters, Orvillise and Wilburta, and their toucan, Richard. Behind them sat the Sultana of Pahang and her hairy elephant, Bye-Bye, and Ottoline's new friend Cecily with Mumbles the pony. At the back sat Newton Knight the Boy Genius and his robot, Skittles.

Ottoline sat down next to Cecily and the
school bus rattled and shuddered as it set off
through the city.

"Have I ever told you about the time I
caught a mermaid?" said Cecily.

"I don't think so," said Ottoline, "but it
sounds fascinating."

They left Big City and drove high into the
mountains.

51

Eventually they came to a large mansion on top of a mountain.

The door of the mansion was opened by an extremely tall butler.

"Well, here we are. Home sweet home!" said Alice B. Smith with a smile. "Solihull will show you to your rooms. Sleep well – school begins tomorrow at thirteen o'clock sharp."

They all followed Solihull the butler up an extremely grand staircase. On the wall were pictures of famous ex-pupils of the Alice B. Smith School for the Differently Gifted.

DOTTIE NEUWORTH, THE OPERATIC YODELLER

BALDY MᶜSTEWART, THE FRIDGE MAGNATE

THE NABOB OF SOB

Solihull showed the pupils to their rooms.

"Your dog has to go with the other pets," said Cecily. "They sleep in the East Wing."

"See you in the morning," said Ottoline to Mr. Munroe.

THE FORBES-LAWRENCE
ROOM

GOODNIGHT

63

THE BOYS'
DORMITORY

GOODNIGHT

THE GIRLS'
DORMITORY

GOODNIGHT

BY HOT AIR BALLOON

Professor & Professor Brown
c/o The Roving Collectors Society

Dear Ma and Pa,

I'm sharing a room with my friend Cecily Forbes-Lawrence III. Her grandmother is called Cecily Forbes-Lawrence I and was an extremely famous opera singer. I haven't discovered my different gift yet,

lots of love,

O

X X X.

P.S. I'm giving this letter to Solihull the butler to deliver to the Society when he does the shopping. Write back soon!

P.P.S. Cecily didn't sleep well. She is worried about Mumbles. She says he is homesick.

65

Chapter Five

The next morning at thirteen o'clock Alice B. Smith showed the pupils the timetable . . .

THE SCHOOL CLOCK

ALICE B. SMITH THINKS DRESSING UP IS VERY IMPORTANT AND THAT THE NUMBER NINE IS UNLUCKY. SHE DOESN'T BELIEVE IN WEDNESDAYS

	MONDAY	TUESDAY	THURSDAY	FRIDAY	THE WEEKEND
LESSON 1	SITTING PRACTICE	LOOKING	GIGGLING STUDIES	USEFUL SKILLS	**P E R S O N A L D E V E L O P M E N T**
LESSON 2	PAPER FOLDING	SEEMING	WEEPING WORKSHOP	USELESS SKILLS	
	LUNCH	PICNIC	BUNFIGHT	BANQUET	
THE AFTERNOON	ADVANCED MUSING	BEING	TEACUP CLASS	WHISTLING CHOIR	
EVENING	FREE TIME				
	BEDTIME				

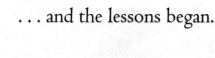

. . . and the lessons began.

MONDAY

SITTING PRACTICE

CORRECT POSTURE WHEN SITTING ON AN OTTOMAN

68

PAPER FOLDING

THE FIVE-FOLD PARTY INVITATION

LUNCH

SOMETHING BROWN AND STRINGY

SOMETHING GREEN AND MUSHY

SOMETHING YELLOW AND LUMPY

ADVANCED MUSING

THINKING ABOUT CLOUDS

OTTOLINE'S NOTEBOOK

Strange noises in the night — MUST INVESTIGATE...

Brian the invisible boy without his clothes!

Advanced Musing is VERY HARD, I think!

69

TUESDAY

LOOKING

EAGLE
SPOTTING

70

IMPERSONATING
A HEDGE

SEEMING

BEING

BEING
A
PRINCESS

PICNIC

SOLIHULL'S JAM AND
FISH PASTE SANDWICHES

OTTOLINE'S
NOTEBOOK

Mr. Munroe thinks my
different gift looks
like this and he is
looking for
it all over
the school!!

Cecily is very good
at being a princess.

73

FRIDAY

USEFUL SKILLS

CONKERS

USELESS SKILLS

BURPI[N]

BANQUET

SOLIHULL'S ← BANGERS AND MASH

WHISTLING CHOIR

[TWINKLE, TWINKLE, LITTLE STAR

Newton Knigh[t] the cleverest in the world, I'm better at burping! Cecily says Mumbles is sti[ll] homesick.

OTTOLINE'S NOTEBOOK

74

On Friday night, Ottoline visited Mr. Munroe in the East Wing.

"I've had such a busy week!" she told him. "Looking lessons and teacup class and paper folding and whistling . . ."

Mr. Munroe had had a busy week too, searching for Ottoline's Different Gift, which he was sure must be somewhere in the school. He had been looking for it that morning when he saw Mumbles the Patagonian pony disappear down a long corridor. Mr. Munroe was about to tell Ottoline this when Cecily interrupted them.

"I hate weekends," complained Cecily. "At weekends we have 'Personal Development'."

"What's that?" asked Ottoline.

"You'll see," said Cecily, "but first you're invited to my slumber party tonight." Cecily looked at Mr. Munroe. "Dogs aren't allowed," she said.

Chapter Six

That night Cecily hosted the slumber party in her five-poster bed.

"You have the nicest room," said Wilburta.

"I know," said Cecily casually, "but I prefer my bedroom at home. It's much bigger . . ." Cecily examined her fingernails. "And besides," she went on, "my bedroom at home isn't haunted."

"Haunted?" everybody exclaimed at once. "The Alice B. Smith School is haunted?"

"Yes," said Cecily with a yawn. "Didn't you know? Once upon a time," she began, "there was a pretty young teacher called Alice Brunhilda Smith, who was best friends with a beautiful opera singer called Cecily. She played piano for Cecily and helped her learn her lines, until Cecily became famous and married a cod-liver-oil tycoon whose brother was a notorious pirate, but that's another story . . .

79

"Anyway, Alice decided to look
for another challenge and set
off in her Armstrong-Siddley
three-wheeler.

"One dark and stormy
Wednesday night the Armstrong-
Siddley broke down on a lonely mountain
road miles from anywhere . . ."

"I'm frightened," said Orvillise.

"Go on," said Ottoline in a whisper.

"Well," said Cecily,

"Alice saw a light
in the distance and
decided to go and ask
for help.

"Alice knocked on the front door and waited.
There was the sound of great heavy footsteps
approaching, the jangling of keys and then
a long creaking squeak as the door slowly
opened . . ."

"I'm frightened," said Wilburta.
"Go on," said Ottoline in a whisper.

"Standing there was a young man with big, clunky shoes and rather wild hair. 'Hello,' he said. 'Welcome to Hammerstein Castle. My name is Hector Hammerstein. How can I help you?'

"'My car has broken down,' said Alice. 'I don't suppose . . .'

"'Leave it to me,' said Hector. 'I'll have Solihull bring it to my laboratory.'

"Just then there was a jagged flash of lightning and a tremendous clap of thunder and a huge monster appeared in the doorway.

"Hector Hammerstein told Alice not to be frightened. The monster's name was Solihull and he was the butler. He'd been created in the laboratory by Hector's father, the mad scientist Dudley Hammerstein. Solihull was very good-natured, Hector explained, and he kept the mansion spick and span. The only frightening thing about Solihull was his love of jam and fish paste sandwiches."

"What about the ghost?" asked the Sultana of Pahang.

"I was just getting to that," said Cecily. "Solihull brought the car to the laboratory and Hector set about fixing it. It took quite some time, but Alice was very impressed.

"'I'm very impressed, Hector,' she said when he'd finished. 'I think you've found your gift . . .' Just then, the clock struck nine o'clock . . ."

I'M FINDING THIS STORY RATHER UNSETTLING...
I'M FRIGHTENED!
I'M SCAR

"When the lights came back on, Alice's car was a wreck. It had been battered and pulverized and was covered in horseshoe-shaped dents.

"'It's the curse of the Horse of the Hammersteins!' exclaimed Hector, turning pale and trembling. 'My father got rid of the family carriage and replaced it with a luxury limousine. The family horse never forgave him. Although it went on to have a very successful career in carriage croquet, it vowed to return and haunt the castle in revenge!'

"'How fascinating,' said Alice.

"'This is the final straw. I've had enough!' said Hector. 'I'm just not cut out to be a mad scientist. I've done the hair and the clunky shoes, but my heart just isn't in it. You can have the mansion. I'm off to Big City for a quiet life!'

"So Hector left and started the extremely successful Hammerstein's Horseless Carriage Repairs Co., and Alice stayed and started her School for the Differently Gifted," said Cecily.

"But on dark, stormy nights, the Horse of the Hammersteins returns to seek revenge for the terrible wrong it suffered, by scaring anyone it finds out of their wits, or worse. . . ."

"Worse?" said Wilburta, Orvillise, Brian, Newton and the Sultana of Pahang.

"Time for bed," Cecily yawned.

Everybody went to bed . . .

. . . but nobody slept well . . .

THE FORBES·LAWRENCE
ROOM

SOB

. . . except for Ottoline.

93

Chapter Seven

"Here at the Alice B. Smith School for the Differently Gifted," said Alice B. Smith the next morning, "we like to encourage our pupils to develop their different gifts."

"Excuse me, Miss Smith," said Ottoline, "but what if someone doesn't have a gift?"

"Nonsense!" said Alice B. Smith with a giggle. "Everyone has some sort of gift or other. It's just a matter of finding it . . ." She turned to the other pupils. "Now, everyone, why don't we show Ottoline what we've been working on?"

In the school hall, Brian the Invisible Boy and his dog, Bodge, demonstrated their remarkable gift for plate spinning.

"Why don't you have a go?" said Alice B. Smith.

Ottoline tried plate spinning . . .

. . . without much success.

97

"Never mind," said Alice B. Smith cheerfully.
"Solihull will find Mr. Munroe a bandage."

In the school gymnasium, the Wright sisters, Orvillise and Wilburta, demonstrated their amazing gift for aerial flower arranging.

99

"Let's see what you can do,"
said Alice B. Smith.

Ottoline tried aerial flower arranging . . .

. . . but she
dropped the
flowers and her
shoe came off.

"Cheer up," said Alice B. Smith after they
had bandaged Mr. Munroe's hand. "Flower
arranging isn't everyone's cup of tea."

In the school dining room, the Sultana of
Pahang demonstrated her extraordinary gift
for curtain origami.

Ottoline tried curtain origami . . . but it was harder than it looked.

Alice B. Smith nodded encouragingly. "Top marks for effort," she said. "By the way, you're standing on Mr. Munroe's toe, dear."

Outside in the school grounds, Cecily
and Mumbles demonstrated their gift
for carriage croquet.

Ottoline and Mr. Munroe tried
carriage croquet . . .

"Good shot!" laughed Alice B. Smith.

"Beginner's luck," said Cecily, taking back her mallet and ball and giving Mr. Munroe a particularly hard stare. "Besides, dogs aren't allowed to play. It's the rules."

In the school art room, Newton Knight the Boy Genius was demonstrating his artistic gifts.

"Newton is the cleverest boy in the world," explained Alice B. Smith. "He finds that painting helps his brain relax."

Ottoline tried
painting . . .

. . . and Mr. Munroe helped with the
paint pots.

"Oops!" 109
said Ottoline.
"Well, that's
certainly
different . . ."
said Alice B.
Smith.

Chapter Eight

A fter lunch, everyone went home with
their parents for Saturday night
and Sunday morning. Everyone except for
Ottoline and Cecily.

CAPTAIN
WRIGHT →

D
KN ←

Ottoline's parents were away on a collecting trip and Cecily's parents were too busy.

THE INVISIBLE MAN

THE SULTAN OF PAHANG

"Of course, it's Mumbles I feel sorry for,"
Cecily said to Ottoline as they walked through
the modern-sculpture garden that afternoon.
"He misses my parents terribly. I wish school
was over and I could take him home."

That night, when Ottoline heard Cecily crying, she got out of bed and tiptoed over to her five-poster bed.

"What is it?" said Cecily, drying her eyes.

"I've got a plan," said Ottoline and she showed Cecily the invitation the bear had packed into her trunk. "It says to bring a friend."

THE CLOTHES
THE BEAR
PACKED

As they sneaked down the extremely grand
staircase, Cecily told Ottoline all about the
time her mother, Cecily Forbes-Lawrence II,
had been a pupil at the Alice B. Smith school
and had discovered a secret tunnel.

"Where?" asked Ottoline as they quietly
opened the big front door and tiptoed out.

"If I told you," said Cecily, "then it
wouldn't be a secret."

Ottoline and Cecily arrived at the Picnic Club and showed their invitation.

The bears certainly knew how to throw a
party. Ottoline and Cecily danced the Grizzly
Hokey Cokey and the Bear-Foot
Stomp . . .

118 They had tea for two, with
twin pots of Canadian
honey . . .

And then danced some more . . . until it was
quite late in the night or very early in
the morning. Ottoline
wasn't sure
which.

Then it began to
rain, and the bears packed
away their picnic and switched
off the lights. The party was over.

By the time Ottoline and Cecily got back
to school it was a wild and stormy night.
Lightning flashed overhead and thunder
cracked.

They silently tiptoed up the extremely grand staircase. From behind them came a *Thump! Thump! Thump!*

"You don't think," said Ottoline, "that it could be the Horse of the Hammersteins, do you?"

"Of course not," said Cecily. But Ottoline could feel her friend trembling as she gripped her hand tightly. "It can't be . . ."

121

Slowly they both turned around and . . .

"I'm sorry I startled you," said Solihull the butler. "Let me hang up those wet jumpers and bring you some hot milk."

"You're not going to tell Miss Smith?" asked Cecily.

"Of course not, Miss Forbes-Lawrence," said Solihull.

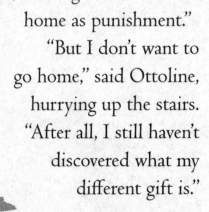

"Pity," muttered Cecily as Solihull lumbered off to the kitchen. "If he did, she might send us both home as punishment."

"But I don't want to go home," said Ottoline, hurrying up the stairs. "After all, I still haven't discovered what my different gift is."

Chapter Nine

BY CAMEL CARAVAN

Professor & Professor Brown,
c/o The Roving Collectors' Society

Dear Ma & Pa,

Hope you are well. Bad news. I still haven't discovered what my different gift is. Mr. Munroe says my painting is interesting, but I don't believe him and the big pot of blue paint I was using has disappeared. Newton Knight the Boy Genius has lost his skateboard, and the Sultana of Pahang's pencil case is missing. As soon as I discover my gift I shall investigate,

lots of love,

O

X X X.

P.S. Solihull told me the weedkiller is missing from the garden shed!

P.P.S. Cecily got a letter from her parents' secretaries, saying her parents will write when they're not so busy!

126

COUNT HAMMERSTEIN & SON

127

PING PONG

THE QUESTING MAID

PAN MACMILIAN

CLIP
CLOP
CLIP
CLOP
CLIP

CLIP
CLOP
CLIP

CLIP
CLOP

CLIP
CLOP

CLIP
CL

AAAAAAAAHHH!

CLIP CLOP CLIP CLOP!

131

The scream came from Cecily. "Look!"
she said, pointing to the portrait of her
grandmother Cecily Forbes-Lawrence I.

"It's the curse of the Horse of the
Hammersteins!" she said dramatically.

"Oh dear," said Alice B. Smith, who had been woken by Cecily's scream and had come to find out what all the commotion was about. "What can it mean?"

"This school is HAUNTED!" said Cecily theatrically. "I think you should send us all home, Miss Smith."

"Such a wonderful imagination, Cecily dear."
Alice B. Smith smiled. "Let's all go back to
bed. Things will look better in the morning."

"I doubt it," said Cecily. "By the way, why
isn't Ottoline's dog in the East Wing?"

Everybody turned and looked at Mr.
Munroe. He was holding a red crayon in
his hand, and at his feet was the Sultana of
Pahang's missing pencil case. He had found
it on the floor outside the Forbes-Lawrence
Room just a moment ago.

"Bad dog!" said Cecily with a smile.

"I'm very disappointed in you, Ottoline," said Alice B. Smith. "Your pet's behaviour is your responsibility. Come and see me in my study tomorrow morning at thirteen o'clock sharp."

CANADIAN
ARCTIC SOCKS
THAT THE
BEAR PACKED

135

Chapter Ten

The next morning at thirteen o'clock, Ottoline and Mr. Munroe went to Alice B. Smith's study.

"As punishment for scribbling on Cecily Forbes-Lawrence I," said Alice B. Smith, "I want you to write out, 'I must supervise my pet more closely'."

"Yes, Miss Smith," said Ottoline. "How many times?"

"Just once," said Alice B. Smith, giving Ottoline a large sheet of paper, "but in very big letters."

Ottoline and Mr. Munroe were in the art room writing out their line in big letters when Mr. Munroe thought he heard something over by the door.

"Stay where you are," said Ottoline, drawing an extra big "SELY". "I've got to supervise you more closely. We'll finish this and then go and investigate together."

A moment later Brian and
Bodge walked in . . .

ART ROOM

"It's the curse of the Horse of the Hammersteins," said Cecily, who just happened to be passing by. "We should all leave now!"

So that's where my blue paint went, thought Ottoline.

"Shouldn't you take your line to Miss Smith?" said Cecily helpfully.

Ottoline and Mr. Munroe exchanged looks . . .

They set off for Alice B. Smith's study and were passing the staircase when Mr. Munroe saw something on the second to top step.

"We'll give this line to Miss Smith and then go and investigate together," said Ottoline.

141

EMERGENCY!
EMERGENCY!

Just then
Newton and
Skittles appeared at
the top of the stairs . . .

142

"MY SKATEBOARD!"
said Newton.

"It's the curse of the Horse of the
Hammersteins," said Cecily, who just
happened to be passing by. "No one is safe!"

Ottoline and Mr. Munroe exchanged looks.

143

They reached Alice B. Smith's study and
Ottoline was about to knock on the door
when they both heard a *snip-snipping* sound
coming from the school dining room.

Mr. Munroe looked at Ottoline.
"We should investigate now," said Ottoline.

"It's the curse," said Cecily, who just happened to be passing by, "of—"

"The Horse of the Hammersteins. I know, I know," said Ottoline.

"It'll only get worse!" warned Cecily.

Just as Mr. Munroe spotted the pruning shears lying on the floor behind a chair leg, two loud screams echoed down the corridor.

Ottoline and Mr. Munroe began to run in the direction of the school gymnasium.

"It's the Horse of the Hammersteins!" Cecily called after them.

Mr. Munroe held up the empty bottle of weedkiller he had spotted in the corner of the gymnasium.

"I think the Horse of the Hammersteins has gone too far this time," said Ottoline. "Don't you?"

Mr. Munroe nodded. "What on earth is all this commotion about?" asked Alice B. Smith.

"We're frightened," said Alice B. Smith's Differently Gifted pupils. "We think the school is haunted!"

Alice B. Smith laughed a tinkling little laugh. "Oh," she said, "the ghosts here at the Alice B. Smith School are all very friendly." She smiled. "I wouldn't let them stay if they weren't. You leave the matter with me. I'm sure there won't be any more trouble."

"Well, if there is," said Cecily firmly, "we shall tell our parents to come and take us home!"

All the Differently Gifted pupils nodded except for Ottoline.

Alice B. Smith gave everyone the rest of the day off to think things over. "You can decide tomorrow morning," she said, "after a good night's sleep."

"I don't suppose the ghost will let us get a good night's sleep, do you?" said Ottoline to Cecily.

The day passed slowly . . .

OTTOLINE LIKED TO BRUSH MR. MUNROE'S HAIR WHEN SHE WAS THINKING UP CLEVER PLANS

CECILY LIKED TO BRUSH MUMBLE'S MANE BEFORE CARRIAGE-CROQUET PRACTICE

OTTOLINE'S NOTE BOOK

CLEVER PLAN.

M.M.

150

. . . until at last it
was bedtime. 151

Everybody climbed into Cecily's five-poster bed.

"If we don't leave the Alice B. Smith School for the Differently Gifted tomorrow," said Cecily with a smile, "then we'll all be DOOMED!"

 "We'll see about that," said Ottoline.

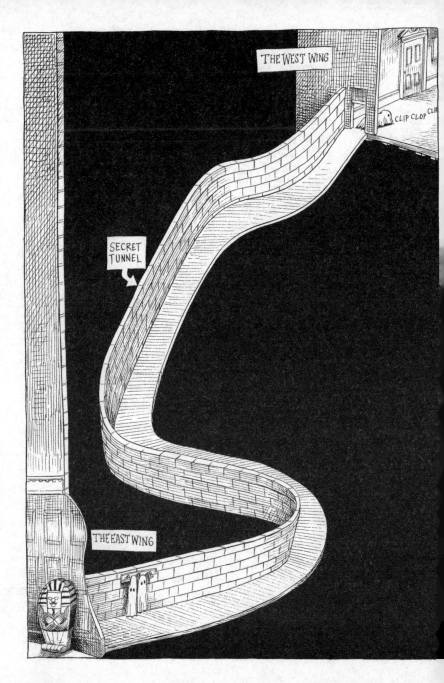

CLIP

CLOP

CLIP

CLOP!

"I can hear something!" whispered Newton.

"So can I," said Brian.

"I'm frightened," said Orvillise.

"Me too!" said Wilburta.

"The ghost is coming!" trembled the
Sultana of Pahang.

"I told you so," said Cecily. "Didn't I,
Ottoline . . . ? Ottoline? Ottoline . . . ?"

GIRLS' DORMITORY

BOYS' DORMITORY

Suddenly some bright lights came on . . .

. . . a beautifully woven floral net dropped . . .

. . . and the ghost was bundled up in an expertly folded parcel.

"It's all right, there's no need to be frightened," said Ottoline to the Alice B. Smith Differently Gifted pupils. "Show them, Mr. Munroe."

Mr. Munroe stepped forward.

He unwrapped the parcel, snipped through the beautifully woven floral net and pulled off the white sheet . . .

WOOF!

162

"Mumbles!" exclaimed Alice B. Smith,
who'd come to see what all the commotion
was about.

The next morning, Alice B. Smith called a special assembly.

"Congratulations, Ottoline," she said. "You've discovered your gift!"

"I have?" asked Ottoline.

"Yes," said Alice B. Smith, pinning a shiny badge to Ottoline's blazer.

ALICE B. SMITH
SCHOOL

DIFFERENT GIFTS

NEWTON
KNIGHT - ROBOT PAINTING

THE SULTANA
OF PAHANG - CURTAIN ORIGAMI

BRIAN
INVISIBLE - PLATE SPINNING

ORVILLISE &
WILBURTA
WRIGHT - AERIAL FLOWER ARRANGING

CECILY
FORBES-
LAWRENCE - CARRIAGE QUET

OTTOL
BROWN

MR.
MUNROE
WAS GIVEN
A BADGE
TOO

164

THIS IS
OTTOLINE'S
BADGE

SPOOK
SPOTTER

ALICE B. SMITH SCHOOL

SPOOK
SPOTTING

DIFFERENT GIFT

Ottoline looked at the badge.

"I couldn't have done it without a clever plan," she said, "and a little help from my friends."

Then, glancing at Cecily, who was looking very sorry and ashamed of herself, she leaned forward and whispered into Alice B. Smith's ear.

Alice B. Smith listened and nodded slowly. "You're right," she said, patting Ottoline on the shoulder. "You really are Differently Gifted, my dear."

165

Professor & Professor Brown,
C/o The Roving collectors'
Society

Dear Ma & Pa,

The school isn't haunted by the Horse of the Hammersteins. It was just one of Cecily's stories. She was homesick but is very sorry for causing a fuss.

Alice B. Smith is sending her home early with a school report. I'm looking forward to showing you mine!

lots of love,

× × ×.

P.S. I found my different gift! Mr. Munroe helped me. He sends his love.

ALICE B. SMITH SCHOOL

REPORT

NAME: MR. & MRS. FORBES-LAWRENCE II

SUBJECT	GRADE	COMMENTS
BEDTIME STORIES	B-	you both tell very good stories when you're not too busy!
QUALITY TIME	D	not enough time spent with Cecily - must do better.
HOLIDAYS	F	you must take more holidays with Cecily - very disappointing.
FUN AND GAMES	F	not enough of either because you're both too busy. must both try harder.
PERSONAL DEVELOPMENT	C-	Cecily thinks you both have potential but only if you change your attitude.

GENERAL COMMENTS:

very disappointing but Cecily and I think that you can both improve as parents if you apply yourselves. We hope you'll do better in future.

alice B. smith

ALICE B. SMITH   HEADMISTRESS

The next day a large fancy car rolled up the drive and Mr. and Mrs. Forbes-Lawrence got out. Solihull showed them to Alice B. Smith's study.

When they came out Mr. Forbes-Lawrence was very red in the face and Mrs. Forbes-Lawrence had tears in her eyes. They both gave Cecily a big hug.

"Enjoy an extra long holiday together," said Alice B. Smith, waving goodbye. "And we'll see you next term, Cecily."

"Goodbye, Cecily," said Ottoline. "See you in the holidays."

"By the Turtle Pool," said Cecily with a smile, "in Pettigrew Park and Ornamental Gardens."

Mr. Munroe gave Mumbles an iced bun he'd saved especially.

"I like Cecily," said Ottoline. "She is my second-to-best friend."

Mr. Munroe didn't say anything. He just squeezed Ottoline's hand.